To:_____

From:_____

Fathers & Daughters

Why Daughters Always Need Their Fathers

Written by Meredith R. Katz

new seasons®

A daughter needs a father...

...who will be there when she
needs him the most.

A daughter needs a father…

...who feels privileged just to be her Dad.

A daughter needs a father…

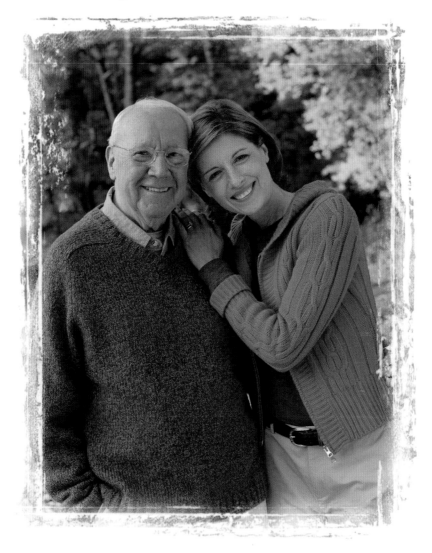

...on whom she can always depend.

A daughter needs a father…

...to teach her that family comes first.

A daughter needs a father...

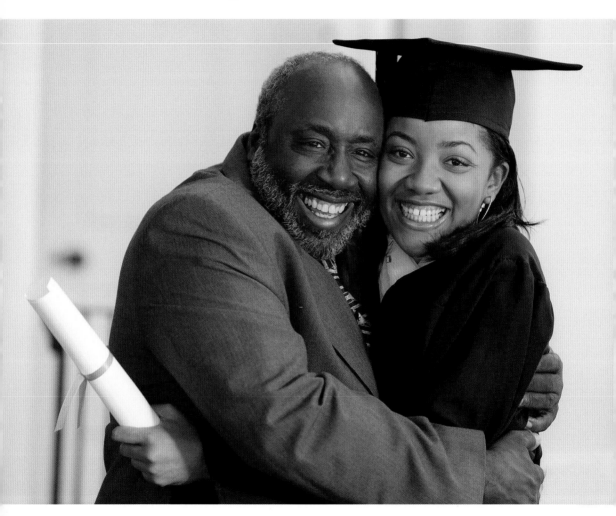

...who knows she will never be
anything less than great.

A daughter needs a father…

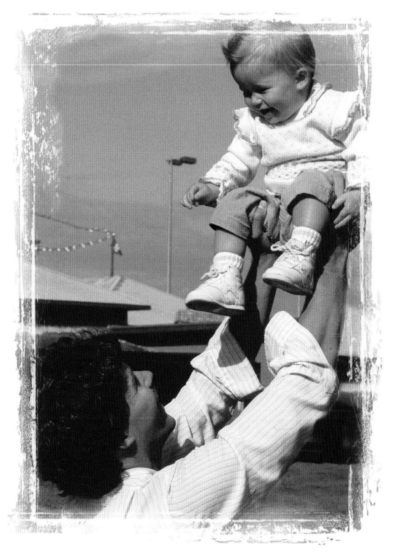

...who considers her to be the light of his life.

A daughter needs a father...

...who will always be her biggest fan.

A daughter needs a father...

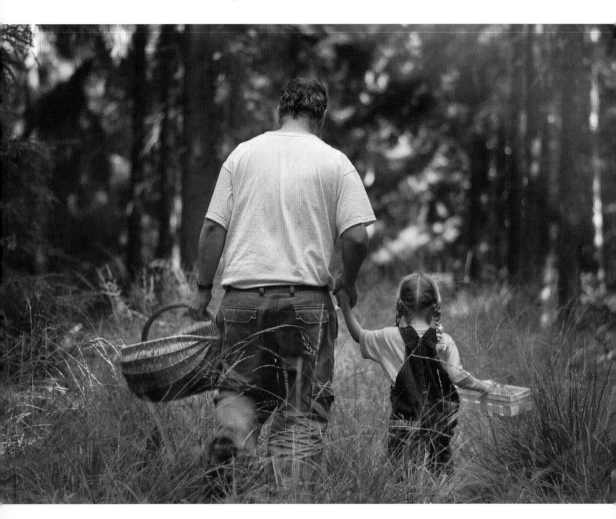

...who encourages her to never stop exploring.

A daughter needs a father...

...who will always keep her protected.

A daughter needs a father…

...to teach her responsibility.

A daughter needs a father...

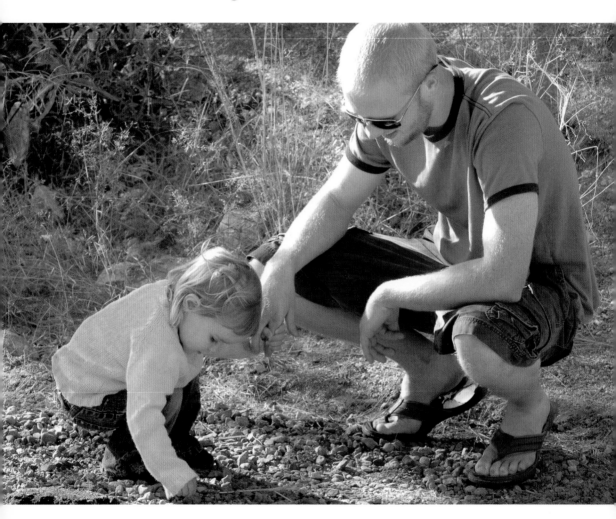

...to answer her questions
as she discovers the world.

A daughter needs a father…

...to teach her the meaning of perseverance.

A daughter needs a father...

...to teach her what she cannot teach herself.

A daughter needs a father…

...who wants "just one more shot,"
to capture the perfect family photo.

A daughter needs a father…

...to be her support when life is unsteady.

A daughter needs a father…

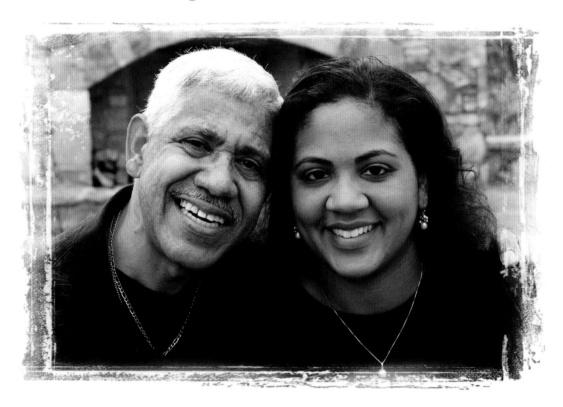

...who will treasure every
moment they have together.

A daughter needs a father…

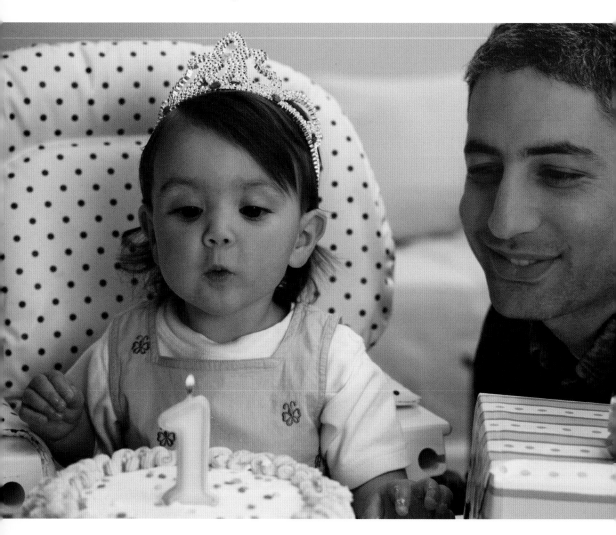

...to help make her wishes come true.

A daughter needs a father...

...who can always make her smile.

A daughter needs a father...

...who makes her feel like the most
beautiful girl in the world.

A daughter needs a father…

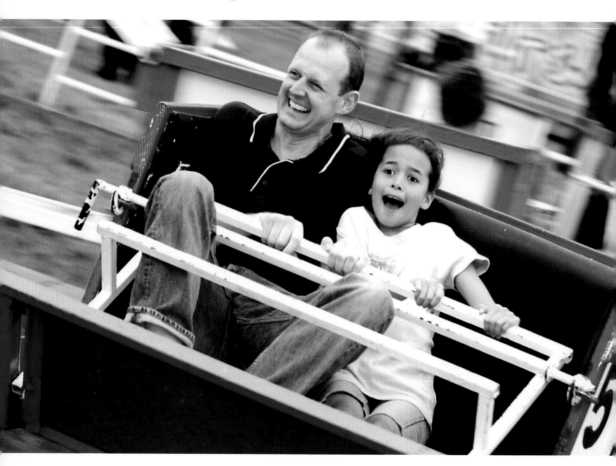

...to make sure she experiences the fun in life.

A daughter needs a father…

...to teach her how to be brave.

A daughter needs a father...

...to help her go the extra mile.

A daughter needs a father…

...who always has time to play.

A daughter needs a father…

...to be her hero.

A daughter needs a father...

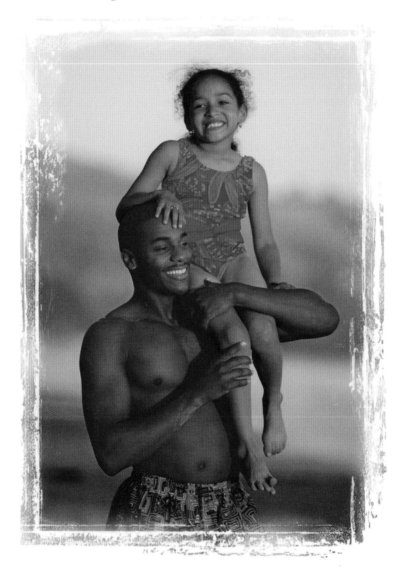

...who will never let her down.

A daughter needs a father...

...who will always be a loving
presence in her life.

A daughter needs a father…

...who makes her an important
part of his family traditions.

A daughter needs a father...

...to teach her patience and understanding.

A daughter needs a father…

...to show her the roots of her family tree.

A daughter needs a father...

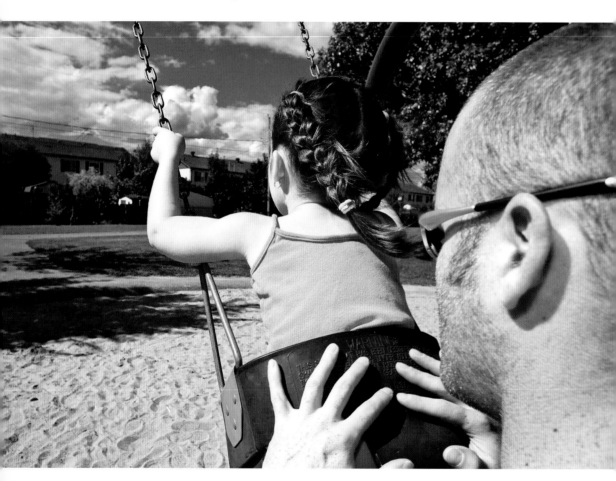

...to push her in the right direction.

A daughter needs a father…

...who is proud of all her accomplishments — big and small.

A daughter needs a father...

...who will give her peace of mind.

A daughter needs a father...

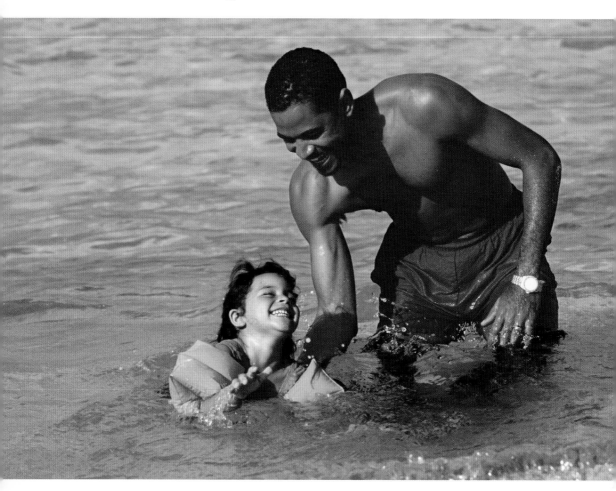

...to make her challenges less scary.

A daughter needs a father…

...who will be there to listen
when she needs to talk.

A daughter needs a father…

...to be her guide when she
forgets which way to turn.

A daughter needs a father...

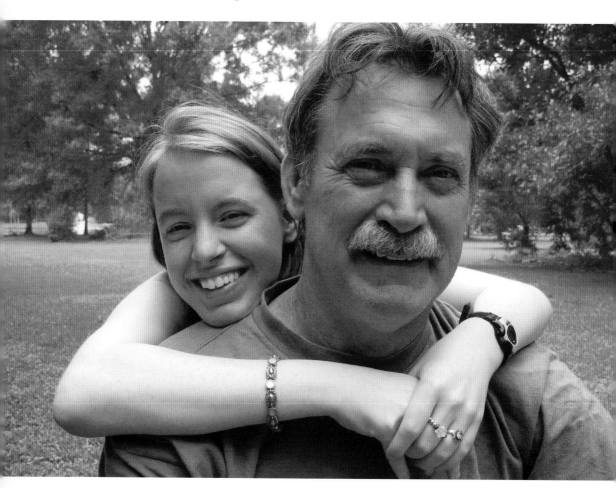

...to remind her that she'll
always be his little girl.